VOLCANOES
AND EARTHQUAKES

written by Don Harper
illustrated by Studio Boni/Galante
and Lorenzo Cecchi

Ladybird

CONTENTS

INSIDE THE EARTH

The Earth is made up of a number of layers. Like an apple, it has a skin called the crust, a flesh called the **mantle** and a core.

Cross section of the Earth

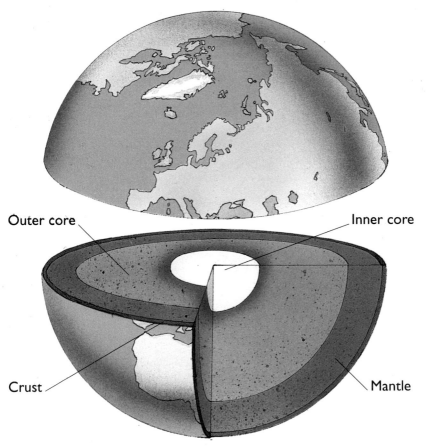

Outer core

Inner core

Crust

Mantle

The Earth's layers

The crust, made of solid rock, has two parts – continental crust and oceanic crust. Beneath the crust is the mantle, made from a layer of hot melted rock, called **magma**. The outer core, is mainly made of nickel and iron and the inner core is mainly iron.

5

THE EARTH'S PLATES

The Earth's crust is in huge pieces called **plates**, which fit together like an enormous jigsaw puzzle. These plates are not still but are constantly moving about, extremely slowly. They may push together, pull apart, or slide past or under each other. Earthquakes and volcanoes are most likely to occur at the plate boundaries. Mountains and trenches also occur where plates meet.

Moving continents
The continents float on the plates and so when the plates move, the continents move too. About 500 million years ago, most of the southern continents were part of one big landmass, called Gondwanaland.

New land and sea
Very gradually, the landmasses drifted apart and came together again. About 175 million years ago, they formed a new continent called Pangaea and a new sea, called Tethys.

Break up of Pangaea
The large landmass of Pangaea began to break up. Over the past 175 million years, very gradually, the continents have drifted apart to where they are now. The continents are still drifting. This makes the Earth 'alive', unlike our Moon, which is said to be dead.

PLATES MOVING APART

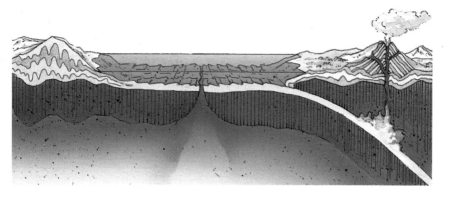

Currents of magma
Molten rock from the mantle pushes up through cracks at plate boundaries in the Earth's crust.

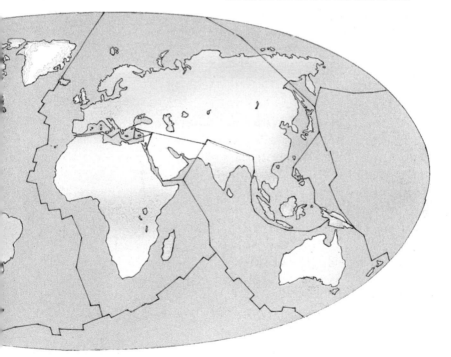

The Earth divided into plates
The plates move extremely slowly each year – about the rate that your fingernails grow.

Satellite pictures show that the Atlantic is growing wider whilst the Pacific is becoming narrower.

WHAT ARE VOLCANOES?

Volcanoes are formed when magma, a mixture of gases, ash and hot melted rock, gushes up from inside the Earth and breaks through a crack or weak spot in the Earth's crust. The magma lies in a **chamber** far below a volcano's **vent**. Pressure builds up, forcing the magma to escape through the vent. Once the magma reaches the surface it is called **lava**.

Lava

Lava is red when hot, turning grey or even black as it cools and hardens on the Earth's surface.

Kinds of volcanoes

Dormant, active and extinct

Around the world, some 800 volcanoes regularly erupt. These are the **active** ones. Others seem to be quietly sleeping or **dormant**. (This comes from a Latin word *dorm*, meaning sleep). A dormant volcano is sometimes mistakenly thought to be **extinct**.

Basaltic volcanoes

These are wide and low, shaped like a shield, and so they are sometimes called shield volcanoes. Dark, runny lava, **basalt**, flows out of basaltic volcanoes, which occur where the Earth's crust is thin, especially at the bottom of the ocean.

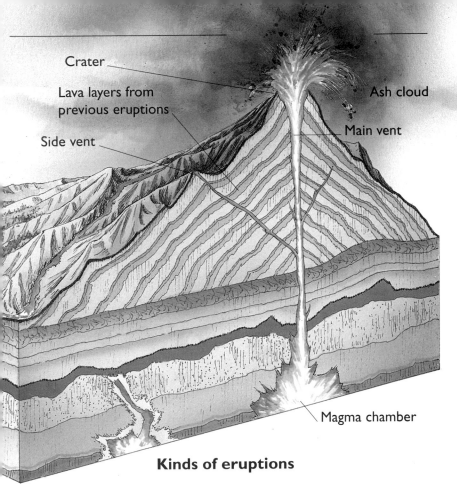

Crater

Lava layers from previous eruptions

Side vent

Ash cloud

Main vent

Magma chamber

Kinds of eruptions

Hawaiian hotspot
Runny lava gently pours out from a volcano with a very wide base.

Vesuvian
Cone-shaped volcanoes that erupt explosively, like Vesuvius in Italy.

Strombolian
Volcanoes that produce huge amounts of volcanic ash and **viscous** lava.

VOLCANOES UNDER THE SEA

More volcanoes are found under the sea than on land because the oceanic crust is thinner than the continental crust. Volcanoes usually occur along the edges of the plates, but some are found in places where the mantle is so hot that it melts a hole in the thin crust above. These are called hotspots. Some of the islands in Hawaii, in the Pacific Ocean, were made by volcanoes forming over a hotspot and erupting under the sea.

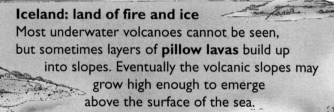

Iceland: land of fire and ice
Most underwater volcanoes cannot be seen, but sometimes layers of **pillow lavas** build up into slopes. Eventually the volcanic slopes may grow high enough to emerge above the surface of the sea.

Hawaii: a chain of volcanoes
As the Pacific plate moves, it carries the volcano formed directly above the hotspot away. This volcano becomes extinct. In this way, a chain of volcanic islands – the Hawaiian islands – is created. An active volcano lies directly above the hotspot and extinct volcanoes beyond it.

New, active volcano forming over hotspot

The new island of Surtsey

In the 1960s a new volcanic island gradually formed off the coast of Iceland. It took about four years for the volcanic rock to pile up above the sea. The new island was named Surtsey after Surt, the Nordic god of fire.

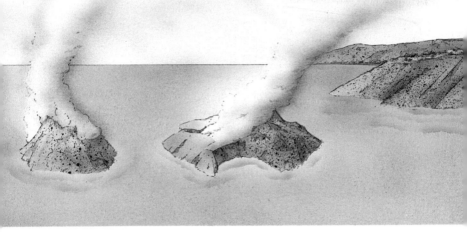

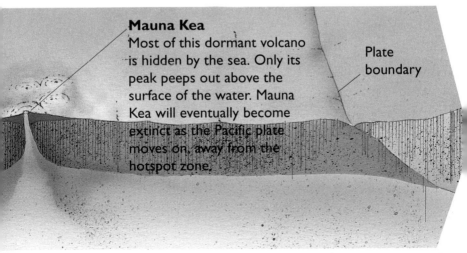

Mauna Kea

Most of this dormant volcano is hidden by the sea. Only its peak peeps out above the surface of the water. Mauna Kea will eventually become extinct as the Pacific plate moves on, away from the hotspot zone.

Plate boundary

VOLCANOES AROUND THE WORLD

Many dramatic and destructive volcanoes have erupted throughout history. Today there are more than 800 active volcanoes on Earth. About 300 of these are in the 'Ring of Fire', around the Pacific Ocean.

Covering of ash
When Mount St Helens, in America, erupted on 18 May 1980, a layer of hot ash covered the surrounding land.

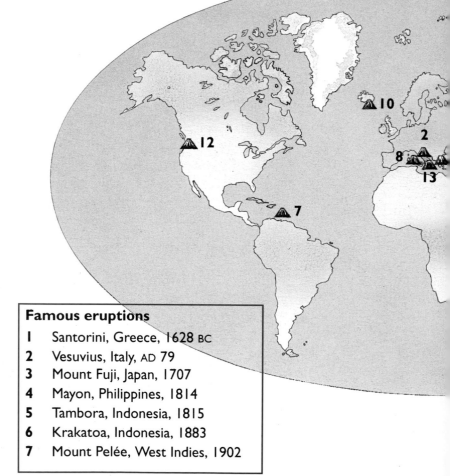

Famous eruptions

1   Santorini, Greece, 1628 BC
2   Vesuvius, Italy, AD 79
3   Mount Fuji, Japan, 1707
4   Mayon, Philippines, 1814
5   Tambora, Indonesia, 1815
6   Krakatoa, Indonesia, 1883
7   Mount Pelée, West Indies, 1902

Destroyed civilisation

In 1628 BC the volcano on the island of Santorini erupted, destroying an early civilisation that was flourishing there.

Big tidal wave

When the volcano erupted on the island of Krakatoa, the island was almost destroyed. The land shook so violently that it caused a gigantic tidal wave.

Changed climate

When Pinatubo, in the Philippines, erupted in 1991, gigantic clouds of dust and gases polluted the air. These drifted around the world, blocking the Sun's heat.

Famous eruptions

8 Stromboli, Italy, 1921
9 Mauna Loa, Hawaii, 1950
10 Surtsey, Iceland, 1963
11 Kilauea, Hawaii, 1971
12 Mount St Helens, America, 1980
13 Etna, Sicily, 1986
14 Mount Pinatubo, Philippines, 1991

VOLCANOES ON OTHER PLANETS

Volcanoes do not just happen on Earth. The biggest volcano in the Solar System is on Mars and is called Mount Olympus. Venus too, has giant volcanoes, created by hotspots deep below the Venusian surface. Maxwell, the tallest Venusian volcano, is nearly two kilometres higher than Mount Everest – our highest continental mountain. Some volcanoes on Venus erupt continuously, pouring out clouds of gas into the flame-coloured sky.

Volcanoes on Io

Sulphur plumes rise from volcanoes on Io, one of Jupiter's moons. A *Voyager* spacecraft found that Io has at least six vents, where gas spurts hundreds of kilometres into space, in shapes that resemble huge umbrellas. Some plumes of gas rise 150 kilometres into the Ioan sky.

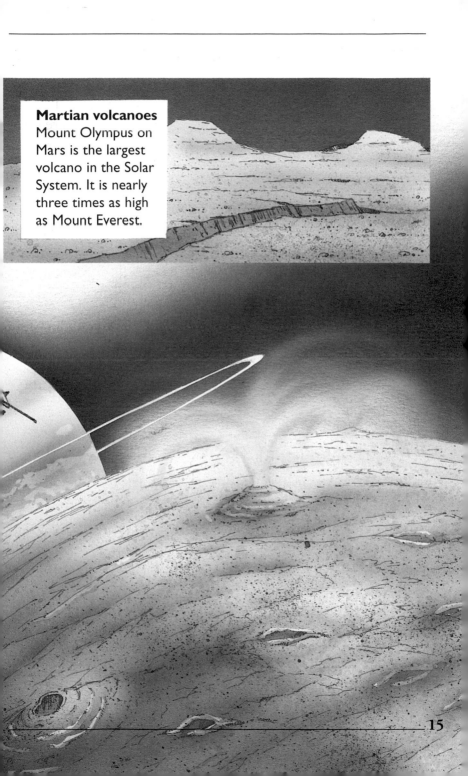

Martian volcanoes
Mount Olympus on Mars is the largest volcano in the Solar System. It is nearly three times as high as Mount Everest.

VOLCANIC ROCKS

When magma from within the Earth pours out of volcanoes – either on land or on the sea floor – as lava, it cools and hardens. Once the lava reaches the surface, it cools quickly and turns into a hard, dark rock, called basalt. As **minerals** in the lava cool, they form tiny crystals. You can see the crystals in basaltic rocks, especially if you use a magnifying glass.

Volcanologists

Studying and measuring volcanoes in action is very exciting and very dangerous. **Volcanologists** wear heatproof suits. Even so, several eminent volcanologists have been killed by surprise, due to an unpredictable eruption.

Rivers of rock

Some molten lava is like a red hot river of rock, setting fire to everything in its path. The lava and ash from volcanoes eventually breaks down and turns into a rich soil, on which plants and trees thrive. Volcanic islands are usually lush and green with plenty of plant life.

The eruption
On 24 August AD 79 Vesuvius began to erupt with terrible force. Hot poisonous gases gushed up, blasting the rock that had been plugging the vent, high into the air. Pompeii was instantly buried under five metres of rock and ash.

THE BURIED CITY

The day that Vesuvius erupted, life in Pompeii came to an instant halt. The volcano blasted hot ash high into the sky, which even blotted out the Sun. Lumps of hot rock rained down on Pompeii, causing raging fires. Thousands of people in Pompeii were suffocated by the poisonous gas and hot ashes that covered the city. Terrified people ran, struggling through the dark streets of Pompeii, towards the sea, to try to escape in boats.

POMPEII

Pompeii was a rich, beautiful and busy city, built in Roman times, on the slope of a mountain called Vesuvius, in Italy. Vesuvius was a volcano that had been dormant for so long that no one thought it would ever erupt again. Crops grew well in the volcanic soil around Vesuvius so the Romans built many villas, farms and grand houses with wonderful views overlooking the sea, on the side of the volcano.

Vesuvius was not as peaceful as everyone thought. It was still active, but a lump of solid rock was blocking its central vent.

area.

gists

h.

in

VOLCANIC ROCKS

Sometimes, magma never reaches the surface of the Earth as lava. Instead, it remains deep down in the Earth, as a magma chamber. Here, the magma cools slowly. Over millions of years the surface rocks are eroded to expose volcanic rock. This kind of volcanic rock is called **granite**. The crystals in granite are large because they had plenty of time to grow.

Pumice
Lava cools to form a very light, frothy rock, with air bubbles trapped in it.

Basalt
Basalt is a dark rock with tiny crystals. It is formed from solidified lava flows.

Granite
Granite is a volcanic rock which has large crystals of feldspar, quartz and mica.

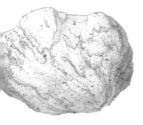

Hidden features
When a very thin slice of rock is looked at under the microscope, in **polarised** light, the shapes and colours of the crystals in the rock are revealed.

A magnified thin section of granite

Feldspar crystal

Quartz crystal

Pyroxene crystal

Olivine crystal

WHY EARTHQUAKES HAPPEN

Most earthquakes occur along great cracks in the Earth called **fault lines**. These are found where one of the Earth's plates is moving against another and building up so much tension that the rock cracks. The sudden crack and movement of the rock sends out shock waves, making the ground shake violently. Every year there are more than one million tiny earthquakes around the world, which cause very little damage. About once every seven years, however there is a huge earthquake.

Cross section of an earthquake

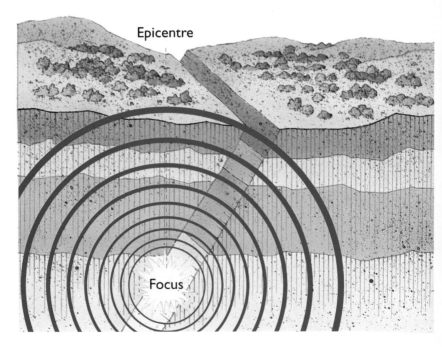

The focus and epicentre

The point within the Earth where the earthquake originates is called the focus. The place on the surface of the Earth, immediately above the focus, which vibrates, is called the epicentre.

THE SAN ANDREAS FAULT

Many earthquakes happen around the edges of the plate under the Pacific Ocean. The most famous earthquake zone is called the San Andreas fault. It is the most active fault line on Earth. The cities of San Francisco and Los Angeles in California, America, are built near the fault line. Terrible earthquakes have happened in both cities. An earthquake that hit San Francisco on 17 January 1994 killed fifty-four people and caused chaos.

WHAT TO DO IN AN EARTHQUAKE

1 Put out any fires
Fires can be more dangerous than the earthquake itself.
2 Don't run about outside
Roof tiles, broken glass or concrete blocks might be falling from buildings.
3 Protect your head
If you can, find a soft pillow or cushion to protect yourself with. The safest place to crouch during an earthquake is inside a door frame.

An early earthquake detector
The earliest known **seismometer** was designed by Chang Heng, in China, in AD 132. It was built around a heavy pendulum, attached to dragon's heads, each of which held a metal ball. At the onset of an earthquake, the pendulum would swing, causing a ball to drop down into a frog. This frog pointed towards the earthquake.

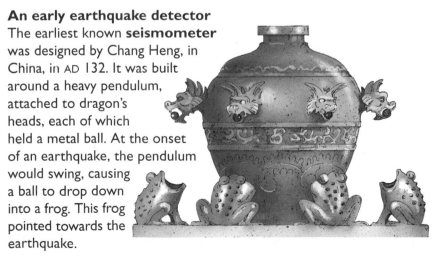

PREDICTING EARTHQUAKES

It is impossible to prevent earthquakes from happening, but scientists, called seismologists, can sometimes predict when and where an earthquake might occur. They use creepmeters, **laser beams** and magnetometers to monitor fault lines that are known to be active, where the Earth's plates are touching or sliding past one another.

A laser beam
Seismologists use laser beams to identify rock movements before an earthquake.

Sensitive animals
Some animals can detect vibrations or changes in the ground, moments before an earthquake happens, giving a warning signal.

Chinese snakes
Prior to the earthquake in Haicheng, China, in 1975, snakes left their burrows.

Japanese catfish
Before the earthquake in Tokyo, Japan, in 1923, catfish jumped out of their ponds.

MEASURING EARTHQUAKES

Instruments called seismometers
measure the size of an earthquake.
The relative force of each earthquake
is recorded on a Richter scale.
Most of the one million tremors that
occur every year only reach 2
on the Richter scale. But
the earthquakes that reach 8
on the scale are powerful
enough to flatten cities.

A Richter scale recording

The Mercalli scale

The intensity of an earthquake can also be measured in terms of
damage caused and the amount of shaking that happens.

2

4

6

8

10

12

SHOCK WAVES

During an earthquake, shock waves of pent-up energy are sent round the Earth. Some shock waves travel through all the layers of the Earth. These waves can be picked up on a seismometer anywhere in the world. They travel like sound waves, in the same way as you push and pull a toy train, to make it move. In an earthquake, the ground ripples up and down like water. This is caused by shock waves that only travel along the surface of the Earth, through solid rock. These waves make the ground rise and fall, like when you pump a wave through a rope.

QUAKEPROOF BUILDINGS

The extent of earthquake damage depends on where the earthquake strikes, the number of people living in the area and the types of buildings found there. Nothing can be done to prevent earthquakes happening, but with careful planning, the amount of damage can be reduced. Buildings in areas known to have earthquakes are specially designed to allow them to sway instead of collapsing. Steel cables or 'jackets' are used to strengthen buildings. Special foundations help to absorb ground movement and reduce shaking.

FAMOUS EARTHQUAKES

LISBON, PORTUGAL 1755

Tens of thousands of people died in this earthquake. Some people were killed when the shaking earth made the buildings collapse. Many more were killed when huge fires then broke out, destroying what was left of the city.

TOKYO, JAPAN 1923

Tokyo, the capital of Japan, is built on a fault line. In 1923, while families were cooking their mid-day meal, an unpredicted earthquake suddenly struck. Wooden houses collapsed without hurting many people. But, a whirlwind of fire followed the earthquake, killing thousands.

TANGSHAN, CHINA 1976

On 28 July 1976 there was an earthquake in Tangshan in China that was one of the greatest natural disasters in history. The city had been built over a gigantic coalmine, with many coal tunnels under the city. When the earthquake struck, all the tunnels collapsed and Tangshan was destroyed. Almost 650,000 people were killed.

ARMENIA 1988

In 1988 an earthquake hit the small country of Armenia. An international rescue effort helped the victims. Specially-trained dogs were used to find people trapped under the rubble. Also, infra-red cameras, that can detect body heat, were used to find people surviving under the rubble of fallen buildings.

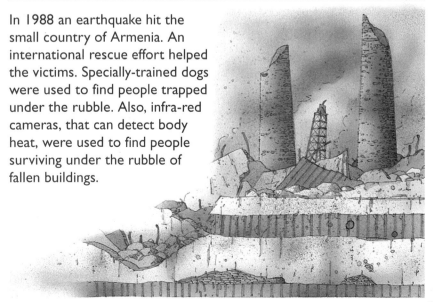

TSUNAMIS

Earthquakes and volcanoes under the sea can sometimes cause a giant wave called a tsunami. A tsunami can be 50 metres tall and destroy everything in its path. They most often happen around the Pacific Ocean, and a warning system has been set up in this area, to predict a tsunami and tell people of the oncoming danger. A tsunami travels at speeds of up to 800 kilometres per hour. This is faster than a jet plane.

Formation of a tsunami
Drop a stone in a river and watch the ripples. The effect is similar to the pattern created by a tsunami and a **seismic wave**. As the sea becomes shallower near the coast, the waves become taller and build up into enormous heights – into waves as tall as tower blocks.

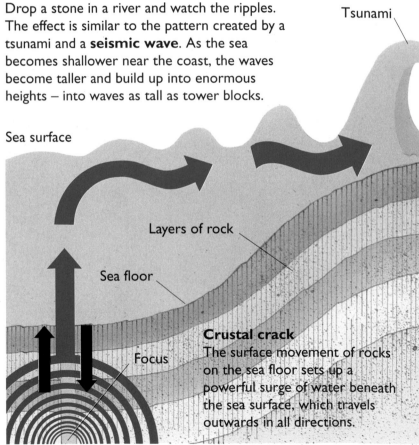

Tsunami

Sea surface

Layers of rock

Sea floor

Focus

Crustal crack
The surface movement of rocks on the sea floor sets up a powerful surge of water beneath the sea surface, which travels outwards in all directions.

HOT ROCKS

Volcanoes and earthquakes sometimes leave small holes or vents in the Earth. Gases from inside the Earth escape through these vents, called **fumaroles**. Hot volcanic rocks can heat water under the ground. The water becomes so hot that it turns into steam and gushes up out of the Earth in a boiling fountain. This is called a **geyser**. Sometimes the heated water bubbles through cracks in the ground and forms hot springs.

Macaque monkeys
Like us, monkeys enjoy bathing in the hot springs found in Honshu, Japan.

AMAZING VOLCANO & EARTHQUAKE FACTS

● **Tsunami** The highest tsunami ever recorded happened off the coast of southern Japan in April 1971. The wave created a great wall of water, 85 metres high.

● **Atlantis** In 1628 BC the volcanic island of Thera (now called Santorini), in Greece, erupted. All life on the island was completely destroyed. People believe that the story of the lost continent of Atlantis, the legendary island in the Atlantic Ocean, developed from stories of the terrible disaster on Santorini.

● **Krakatoa** When Krakatoa erupted, the noise made by the explosion was so loud that it was heard by people living in Australia, more than 7,500 kilometres away. It made the loudest noise ever recorded.

● **Detecting volcanoes** There are likely to be one million detectable signs of volcanic activity each year. Out of these, only about 1,000 eruptions cause any serious damage.

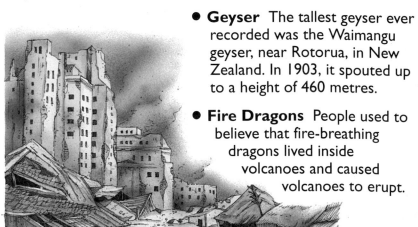

● **Geyser** The tallest geyser ever recorded was the Waimangu geyser, near Rotorua, in New Zealand. In 1903, it spouted up to a height of 460 metres.

● **Fire Dragons** People used to believe that fire-breathing dragons lived inside volcanoes and caused volcanoes to erupt.

GLOSSARY

Active A volcano which has erupted at least once in the past 10,000 years.

Basalt A volcanic rock that is dark and hard and is composed of tiny crystals.

Chamber The area deep within a volcano where hot, molten rock is found.

Dormant A volcano which has not erupted recently.

Extinct A volcano which is thought to be dead.

Fault line A crack in the Earth's surface, which may result in valleys or mountains being formed.

Fumarole A vent in a volcano through which steam and other gases are released.

Geyser A spring of hot water, heated in the depths of the Earth, which spurts up at regular intervals, like a fountain.

Granite A volcanic rock, with large crystals, that has cooled deep in the Earth.

Laser beam Straight line of light, which can be used to measure distances accurately.

Lava The very hot, melted rock ejected from a volcano.

Magma Molten rock in the Earth, which is ejected to form lava.

Mantle The area of the Earth separating the outer crust and the inner core.

Mineral A crystal which makes up rocks. A mineral is formed naturally in the Earth.

Pillow lava Pattern of lava produced by underwater volcanoes.

Plate A part of the outer layer of the Earth which moves very slowly. There are eight major plates, and other minor ones.

Polarise Light waves being transmitted in one direction

Seismic wave A wave caused by an earthquake.

Seismometer An instrument that measures movements of the ground.

Vent The passageway up and out of a volcano, through which the magma erupts.

Viscous Lava that does not flow freely.

Volcanologist A scientist who specifically studies and measures the Earth's volcanic activity.

INDEX *(Entries in **bold** refer to an illustration)*